NOV 1 6 2017

Crazy Crayons

The Sound of CR

By Marv Alinas

2

I like crayons.

I use crayons to make crafts.

I use crayons to draw lines that cross.

I use crayons to draw a crab.

I use crayons
to draw a crown.

I use crayons
to draw a crack.

I use crayons to draw a crib.

15

I use crayons to draw a creek.

18

I use crayons to draw crusty bread.

I can be crazy
with my crayons!

Word List:

crab   creek

crack   crib

crafts   cross

crayons   crown

crazy   crusty

Note to Parents and Educators

The books in this series are based on current research, which supports the idea that our brains are pattern-detectors rather than rules-appliers. This means children learn to read easier when they are taught the familiar spelling patterns found in English. As children encounter more complex words, they have greater success in figuring out these words by using the spelling patterns.

Throughout the series, the texts allow the reader to practice and apply knowledge of the sounds in natural language. The books introduce sounds using familiar onsets and *rimes*, or spelling patterns, for reinforcement.

For example, the word *cat* might be used to present the short "a" sound, with the letter *c* being the onset and "_at" being the rime. This approach provides practice and reinforcement of the short "a" sound, as there are many familiar words made with the "_at" rime.

The stories and accompanying photographs in this series are based on time-honored concepts in children's literature: well-written, engaging texts and colorful, high-quality photographs combine to produce books that children want to read again and again.

Dr. Peg Ballard
Minnesota State University, Mankato

Published by The Child's World®
1980 Lookout Drive • Mankato, MN 56003-1705
800-599-READ • www.childsworld.com

PHOTO CREDITS
© bogdan ionescu/Shutterstock.com: cover, 2; marekuliasz/Shutterstock.com: 6; Mary Swensen: 9, 10, 13, 14, 17, 18; Phase4Studios/Shutterstock.com: 5, 21

Copyright © 2018 by The Child's World®
All rights reserved. No part of this book may be reproduced or utilized in any form or by any means without written permission from the publisher.

ISBN 9781503819344
LCCN 2016960519

Printed in the United States of America
PA02337

ABOUT THE AUTHOR

Marv Alinas has lived in Minnesota all her life. When she's not reading or writing, Marv enjoys spending time with her husband and dogs and traveling to interesting places.